MY FAMILY

BY GINA AND MERCER MAYER

Originally published in a different format by Reader's Digest.

www.littlecritter.com

Printed in the United States by Bookmasters, Inc.
30 Amberwood Parkway, Ashland, OH 44805
January 2013 Job# M10329

Published by FastPencil PREMIERE
3131 Bascom Ave. Suite 150, Campbell CA 95008
Premiere.FastPencil.com

IT'S MINE

BY GINA AND MERCER MAYER

My baby brother wanted to sleep
with my teddy bear.
I said, "No, it's mine."
Mom said, "Why don't you share
with your brother?"

I had to let my brother sleep with my bear even though it's mine.

When I was eating a Popsicle, my dad
asked, “May I have a bite, please?”
I said, “But it’s mine.”
Dad said, “It’s nice to share.”
He took a *big* bite.

I set up my train. My sister wanted to
play with it. I said, “No, it’s mine.”
Mom said, “Let her play, too.”

My sister took the track apart.

My sister was reading my favorite book.
I said, "That book is mine." Mom said,
"She won't hurt it."
I had to let my sister finish reading it.

Then I hid the book under my bed.

My sister was drinking out of my special cup. I took it away. Dad said, "Let her finish her drink."
I said, "But that's my cup."
Dad said, "Nice critters share."

So I fixed myself a drink in
my sister's special cup.
She didn't like that, but Dad told
her, "You have to shar[illegible] too."

I went outside to play in the sandbox.
My sister wanted to play, too.
I said, "No, this is my sandbox."

Mom made me go inside.

I was playing with my building blocks.
My sister wanted to play with them, too.
I said, "No, they're mine."
Dad said, "There are enough blocks
for both of you."

I let my sister play. She knocked
my building down by accident.

So I made a dinosaur with my modeling clay instead. Then my sister wanted to play with the clay.

I said, "This is my clay."
Mom said, "If you don't share,
you will have to put it away."
I shared with my sister.
She made a dumb-looking bunny.

When I was blowing bubbles,
my baby brother wanted to
blow bubbles, too.
I said, “No, these are my bubbles.”
Mom said, “Share!”

He dropped the bottle.

My sister wrapped her doll up in my blanket. I took my blanket back.

She cried.

Mom said, "You don't even
like that blanket."
So I gave it back.
Mom said, "It's nice of you to share."

I caught a big frog in the ditch.
I showed it to my sister.
"Do you want to share?" I asked her.

She said, “Ugh!”
and she ran away.

I guess she didn't want to share my frog.

Well, at least I tried.

JUST LIKE DAD

BY GINA AND MERCER MAYER

When I grow up, I want to be just like my dad.

I'll be able to hit the baseball right out of the park, just like Dad.
Well, at least I'll be able to hit it.

I'll have a big garden, just like Dad.
This is *my* garden.
Maybe I'll remember to water it
when I'm just like Dad.

I'll have a great job, just like Dad.
I'll have a briefcase, too. But I'll play video games on my computer all day long.

When I grow up, I'll be able to drive a car,
just like Dad.
Now he lets me sit on his lap and pretend to drive.

I'll be a great cook, just like Dad.
He cooks lots of eggs.

I’ll have my own money, just like Dad.
My dad says he hopes I have a lot more.

When I grow up, I'll be able to climb a ladder
to wash the windows, just like Dad.
I won't even fall.

And I'll be able to build a fence, just like Dad.
I'll know how to use a hammer and a
screwdriver and everything.

I'll be able to cut the grass with the tractor, just like Dad. He says he can't wait until I can do that.

When I grow up, I'll be able to paint the shutters, just like Dad. And I won't ever get yelled at when I make a mess.

I'll be able to watch anything I want on TV, just like Dad. But I won't ever watch the news.

I'll take showers instead of baths, just like my dad. When I'm just like him, I won't want to play with my tub toys anymore. Maybe.

When I grow up, I'll be able to shave,
just like Dad. I'll be really careful not to get cut.

And I'll wear cologne, just like Dad.
Then Mom will think I smell good, too.

I'll be able to go grocery shopping,
just like Dad. I'll buy anything I want.
I won't even have to ask.

And I'll eat a bowl of cereal every night before bed, just like Dad. Only I won't eat the kind he eats.

When I grow up, I'll be handsome, just like Dad. He's the most handsome critter in the whole world.

But most of all I'll be a great dad,
just like my dad.

Then when my little critters grow up,
they'll want to be just like me.

JUST TOO LITTLE

BY GINA AND MERCER MAYER

My little sister wants to do everything I do, but sometimes she's just too little.

I was playing with my racetrack.
My little sister said, “Can I play, too?”
I said, “No, you’re too little.”

She wanted to play with my marbles,
but I said, "You're too little for marbles."

So she asked to play with my
Super Critter video game instead.
I said, "You're too little for that, too."

Mom said, "She's not too little for everything."
So I let my sister play with my truck.
The wheel was broken anyway.

When my friends came over, they wanted to play cops and robbers. My little sister wanted to play, too. I said, “You’re too little.”

We hid until my
sister went inside.

We had a race.
My sister said, "Can I race, too?"
I said, "You're too little."
She said, "Please?"
So we let her say, "On your mark.
Get set. Go!"

We made a spaceship out of a big
paper box and played astronaut critters.
My sister said, “Can I play?”
I said, “You’re too little to go to the moon.”

But we let her help us land.

When we were skateboarding,
my little sister said, “Can I skate, too?”
I let her try.

She fell down and hurt her knee.
I knew she was just too little.
Mom had to fix up her knee.

We climbed high up in a tree.
My sister said, "Can I come up?"
I said, "You're too little to
come up this far."

So I helped her climb up
on a low branch.

We wanted to walk to the store to get a snack. I knew my little sister was too little to go. We had to sneak away.

But I brought her back some bubble
gum. She got it in her fur.
I guess she's just too little for gum.

Then we tried to catch tadpoles in the ditch.
My sister said, "Can I catch some, too?"
I thought she was too little, but I
let her anyway.

She fell in the ditch and got all muddy.
We took her in the house to get cleaned up.
I knew she was too little.

I played tag with my friends.
My sister said, “Can I play tag?”
I said, “You’re too little.”
We let her sit at home base and watch.

Then we decided to play baseball with some other critters in the park. But we needed one more person to play. My sister said, “Can I play?”

I said, “But you’re too little.”
Mom said, “Let her play.”
I made her play on the other team.

She hit a home run!

My sister is too little to do most
of the things that I like to do.
But she's not too little to play
on my team…next time.

I DIDN'T MEAN TO

BY GINA AND MERCER MAYER

Sometimes I do things
I don't mean to do.

I didn’t mean to knock my sister down.
I guess I was running too fast.

I didn't mean to forget my lunch box.
I was just in a big hurry this morning.

Aa
Bb
Cc
Dd
Ee
Ff
Gg
Hh
Ii

I didn’t mean to step on the cat.
I didn’t know she was there.

I didn't mean to lose my shoe.
It just came off when I kicked my ball.

I didn't mean to rip my jacket.
I was just climbing the fence.

I didn't mean to not wipe my feet.
I didn't know they were so muddy.

Oops! Did I drop my gum in the yard?

Sorry! I didn't mean to.

I didn't mean to be so messy.
I was trying to make a special snack.

I didn't mean to knock
that vase off the table.
I forgot we weren't supposed
to play Frisbee inside.

I didn't mean to scare my brother.
I was only playing.

I didn't mean to pour the whole
bottle of catsup on my hotdog.
It just came out too fast.

I didn't mean to jump on the bed. Well, I guess I really *did* mean to do that.

I didn't mean to break my sister's tricycle.
I was just playing mechanic.

I didn't mean to get glue on the table.
I was making a card for Mom.

I didn't mean to let
my juice fall over.
I thought it would be
fine sitting there.

I didn't mean to
sit on Dad's hat.
I fixed it for him.

I didn't mean to spill the whole bag of chips.
I was just trying to open them for my sister.

I do a lot of things I don't mean to do.
But my mom doesn't *really* get mad at me.
She just tells me to be more careful.

Giving my mom a big hug is
something I always mean to do.

TOMATOES